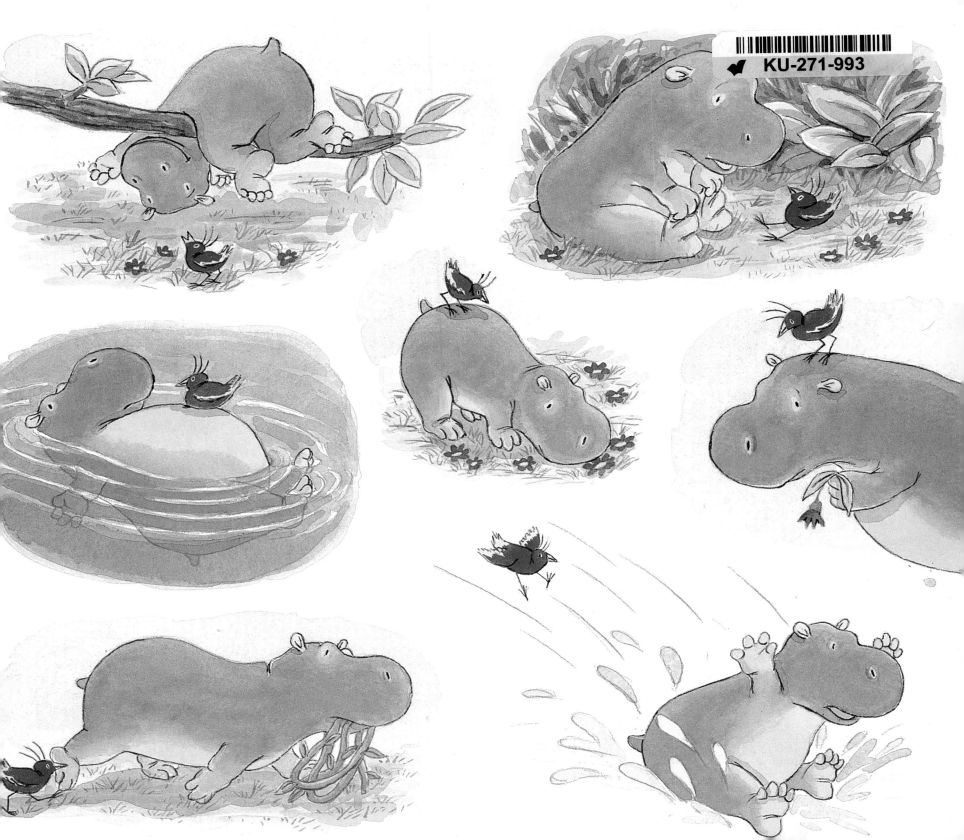

LITTLE TIGER PRESS
An imprint of Magi Publications
22 Manchester Street, London W1M 5PG
This paperback edition published 1999
First published in Great Britain 1999
Text © 1999 Jonathan Shipton
Illustrations © 1999 Sally Percy
Jonathan Shipton and Sally Percy have asserted their
rights to be identified as the author and illustrator of this
work under the Copyright, Designs and Patents Act, 1988
Printed in Belgium by Proost NV, Turnhout
All rights reserved · ISBN 1 85430 614 6
1 3 5 7 9 10 8 6 4 2

or before

THIS LITTLE TIGER BOOK BELONGS TO:

_____

_____

_____

_____

How to be a
Happy Hippo

by Jonathan Shipton   illustrated by Sally Percy

LITTLE TIGER PRESS
London

There was something wrong with Horace.
He had everything a small hippo could
possibly need.
Mountains of food . . .
lots of playthings . . .
and plenty of mud!

But Horace wasn't a happy hippo.
There was something missing from his life.
But he wouldn't tell his sister what it was.
He wouldn't even tell his mum.
And as for his dad . . .

Well, you would have to catch Horace's dad first!
He always had someone to meet,
or somewhere else to go.
So Horace didn't get to see him much.

Sometimes Horace *heard* his dad . . .
He even smelt him once in a while . . .
And, if there was a blue moon, he sometimes got a kiss at bedtime. But all this wasn't enough for a growing hippo.

Horace wanted to learn about crocodiles,

and how to walk along the bottom of
rivers without anyone noticing,

and how to hold his breath.

But, most of all, he just wanted a good
long wallow with his big round dad!

Poor Horace! He tried very hard to catch his dad . . .

but he had no luck at all!

Whatever Horace did, Mr Hippo just wouldn't stop.
There was always someone to see or somewhere to go.
Horace got more and more fed up.

Then, one morning, when Horace
asked him to play, Mr Hippo surprised
everyone by saying, "OK!"
"Yippee!" cried Horace, and he gave his
dad a big hug and asked him, "When?"
Mr Hippo scratched his ear and said,

"Hmm, I think I can manage this afternoon."
Then off he rushed to work.

Horace was so excited he nearly burst!
He spent the morning getting everything ready.
He could hardly wait for his dad to come home.
What a happy hippo Horace was!

He waited and he waited.
He waited until the sun set.
He waited until the first star began to shine.
But still there was no sign of Mr Hippo.

When Mrs Hippo came to look for her little son,
she didn't have to ask him what was wrong.
Poor Horace was so fed up there was only one
thing he could do.

He waited until all the big hippos
had gone to bed.
Then he tiptoed off down the jungle
path in the pouring rain.

Halfway along the path Horace stopped.
He drew a circle in the mud and then he began to dig.

And when the hole was really good and deep,
he scrambled out and carefully covered the top with
sticks and grass and leaves. Then he crept back
home again and fell fast asleep.

The next morning began with a loud
CRASH!
All the hippos rushed out, but Horace
was the quickest.

In fact, he was a bit too quick!
Before you could say,
"Help, Heavy Hippopotamus!"
Horace had fallen into his own hippo trap,
right on top of his . . .

big round dad!
Mr Hippo looked at Horace,
and Horace looked at Mr Hippo.
Mr Hippo rubbed the dirt from
his eyes and snorted . . .

and then he burst out laughing.
He laughed and laughed
and laughed.

He picked up a great big wodge of sticky mud and threw it at Horace.
So Horace picked up an even bigger wetter wodge and chucked it back!

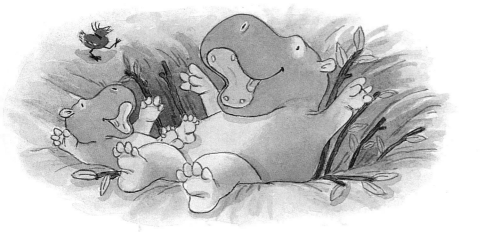

It must have been
wonderful mud, because
they carried on all morning.
You never saw such a pair
of happy hippos!

After lunch Horace and his dad rolled on their backs and chatted about big round hippo things like underwater bubbles and hairy legs, and how to walk along river beds.

And then they did everything, all over again until . . .

the moon rose and the first star came out.
By this time Horace was so tired that Mr Hippo
had to carry him home to bed.

As he was tucking Horace up, the little hippo opened
one sleepy eye and smiled at his big round dad.
"I can't wait till tomorrow," he whispered.
"Neither can I!" whispered Mr Hippo back.

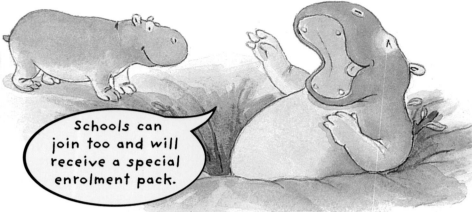

Join the LITTLE TIGER CLUB now for lots more books to enjoy!

Schools can join too and will receive a special enrolment pack.

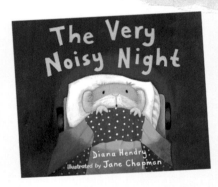

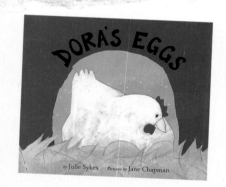

Join the LITTLE TIGER CLUB now and receive a special Little Tiger goody bag containing badges, pencils and more! Once you become a member you will receive details of special offers, competitions and news of new books. Why not write a book review? The best reviews received will be published on book covers or in the Little Tiger Press catalogue.